Timmy
in
Trouble

Timmy in Trouble

Holly Webb

Illustrated by Sophy Williams

SCHOLASTIC INC.

New York   Toronto   London   Auckland
Sydney   Mexico City   New Delhi   Hong Kong

For Eddie and Jamie—keep writing!

ISBN 978-0-545-23281-4

12 11   13 14 15/0

Printed in the U.S.A.   40
First Scholastic printing, November 2010

Chapter One

"How's yours coming along, Katie?" Dad asked.

"I'm just thinking . . ." Katie doodled in the corner of her Christmas present list. A little dog's face, with big, long ears and round, dark eyes. She smiled to herself. He was cute!

"Well, it's only four weeks until Christmas," Dad pointed out. "Both of your grandmothers want to know what to get you. You'll end up with socks if you don't give them some ideas."

Katie's list wasn't very long. Just a couple of books, some new sneakers, and a cell phone, which she knew she wouldn't get because her mom thought she was too young.

"Is that all?" her dad asked in surprise, looking over her shoulder.

Katie looked at him thoughtfully. Was now the right moment to ask?

Dad glanced over at Jess's list. Katie's older sister was sitting on the other side of the table, and her list was enormous. It was also very messy. "I can't read any of that!" he complained. "You'll have to rewrite it, Jess."

Jess looked down at her paper and

grinned. "It's not my fault. Misty kept coming and sitting on it. You know what she's like! I had to write around her."

Misty the cat stopped licking her paws when she heard her name, and looked at them all innocently. *Who me?* she seemed to be saying. She adored pieces of paper, and if anyone was writing or reading a newspaper, she was never happy until she was sitting right in the middle of the page.

Jess leaned across the table to look at Katie's list, too. "You're not getting a phone," she pointed out. "Mom won't even let *me* have one. You can't only want a pair of sneakers."

"Sounds like a nice, easy Christmas shopping trip," Mom said, coming into the kitchen.

Katie smiled hopefully. She'd only put the phone on the list so her parents would say no, and then they'd be more likely to say yes to what she *really* wanted. "So I can't have a phone?" She sighed.

"Absolutely not!" her mom said.

"Oh," Katie said, crossing it out. She tried to sound disappointed, but it wasn't very convincing. "Well, there is one other thing . . ."

Her dad folded his arms, smiling at

her. "I knew it! Break it to me gently, Katie. What is it, an elephant?"

Katie smiled back. "Not quite. But . . . it is an animal." She took a deep breath. "I really, really want a pet."

Mom and Dad exchanged a thoughtful glance, and Jess stopped chewing her pen and sat up straight.

"A pet! We can't have another cat; what about Misty? She'd hate it."

Katie shook her head. "I know. I don't want a cat. I want a dog. A puppy. That's what I'd absolutely, definitely, more-than-anything like for Christmas. Please?" she added, smiling as sweetly as she could at her dad. She knew how much he loved dogs. . . .

"I'm not sure it's a very good idea, Katie," Mom said slowly. She looked at Misty, who'd gone back to washing herself. "Jess, please don't let Misty sit on the table. Her paws are dirty."

"They can't be. She spends all of her time washing them!" Jess pointed out. "Anyway, she'll just jump up again when you aren't looking, Mom."

Mom picked Misty up and tickled her under the chin. "Not on the table, Misty," she said firmly.

Misty stared at her, waiting until she turned around. Then she leaped straight back up again. Katie, Dad, and Jess giggled, and Mom peered over her shoulder and sighed. "I think I'll just pretend I didn't see that," she muttered.

"Mom, why isn't it a good idea?" Katie asked pleadingly. "It would be wonderful to have a dog. You can train dogs," she added persuasively. "I'm sure a dog would be better behaved than Misty!"

Misty glared at Katie, then jumped onto Jess's lap. "Misty's very well behaved," Jess protested, stroking her gently.

"Anyway," Jess continued, "I don't think Misty would like us having a dog. She hates dogs. Remember how upset she got when Meg from next door got under the fence? She hid up at the top of the apple tree for hours!"

Mom nodded. "I know. Misty might not be happy. We'd have to pay extra attention to her. And who'd look after this dog when the two of you are at school? Me, I suppose!" But she was smiling.

"Well," Dad said, "if we did get a puppy, we'd definitely have to be careful. We'd have to introduce the puppy to Misty slowly, so they'd get used to each other." Dad smiled thoughtfully. "I had a dog when I was your age. It was great fun—we went on lots of walks together, in the park and down to the woods. And now that you're eight, Katie, I think you're old enough to help care for a puppy, feeding it and grooming it. Having something to look after would help you be more responsible."

"You mean we *can* get a puppy?" Katie cried, jumping up excitedly and nearly knocking her chair over.

"No," Dad said firmly. "I mean we'll think about it. Not no, but not yes. We need to think it through very carefully. It's not something you can just decide in a moment."

But Katie had seen the wistful look in her dad's eyes when he was remembering those walks with his dog. And she was almost sure that he really meant yes.

Chapter Two

Dad refused to say anything else about dogs that weekend. Katie tried asking a couple of times if he and Mom had had time to think about it yet, but she didn't want to get on his nerves right now. She couldn't believe that they actually might be getting a puppy! She'd hoped, of course, but hadn't really expected them to say yes, or even half yes. It was so exciting!

She spent Sunday afternoon looking at her favorite dog websites on the computer, wondering what sort of puppy they might be able to get, and reading all the advice for new dog owners. There was an awful lot to learn. Especially if you already had another pet, like Misty.

Katie dreamed of dogs that night. She was running through the woods with a gorgeous puppy, just like Dad had described. When she woke up she had a huge smile on her face, although she couldn't quite remember what the puppy had looked like. *Brown and white*, she thought vaguely, *with big, floppy ears*. But she could remember his happy, excited little bark and the soft feel of his springy fur under her hand. It was a wonderful dream. And it might, just possibly, be about to come true!

She was still smiling as she wandered downstairs for breakfast, with her school uniform wrinkled and her curly hair full of tangles.

Mom took one look and sent her back upstairs. "Brush your hair, Katie, for goodness' sake. And put it in pigtails; you've got PE today, remember." She smiled. "I'd hurry up, if I were you. Dad and I have got something to tell you both!"

Katie raced back up to the bathroom. As she galloped up the stairs, she could hear Jess asking what was going on.

Less than two minutes later, Katie was back. Her hair was in pigtails, although the bands didn't match and one was higher than the other. "What is it? What do you want to tell us?" she gasped as she dashed into the kitchen.

Dad chewed a mouthful of cereal very, very slowly, and winked. He was obviously enjoying keeping them in suspense.

Mom shook her head. "Don't tease Katie, Gareth! It isn't fair!" She gave Jess a slightly anxious look as she said it.

"Okay, okay!" Dad put down his cereal bowl and beamed at Katie. "Yes."

"Yes? Really?" Katie jumped up and down excitedly and ran to hug her dad. "When? This Christmas? We're getting a puppy for Christmas?"

"But you can't!" Jess cried. She pushed her plate away and stood up. "You just can't, Dad! What about Misty? Katie can't look after a dog, anyway! And what about all those commercials on TV about not giving dogs as presents? *A dog is for life, not just for Christmas.* All those poor puppies get abandoned every year. It's wrong!"

Dad nodded seriously. "I know, Jess, sit down. You, too, Katie. I haven't finished explaining."

Jess sat down, looking worried, and Katie sat, too, though she was so happy she could hardly keep still.

Dad leaned toward them. "We're not giving you a puppy for Christmas, Katie—"

Katie's eyes opened wide with horror.

"But you said . . ."

"We are getting a puppy, but he or she will be a family dog. Like Misty's a family cat, Jess. You're right that Katie's too young to have all the responsibility of a dog by herself." Dad smiled at Katie. "There's a lot of responsibility, so don't worry, there'll still be plenty for you to do."

Katie felt like butting in and saying that she was sure she *was* old enough, but she decided it was best not to.

Mom leaned over to touch Jess's hand. "Try not to worry, Jess. We know we're going to need to be really careful when Misty meets the puppy. We'll all do our best to make sure she doesn't get upset."

"And we won't bring the puppy home on Christmas, Katie," Dad added.

"We're going to try and get one before Christmas, if we can, or maybe afterward. Christmas is just too busy—it's not a good time to bring a new dog into the house. Mom and I have agreed we'll look around for someone with puppies for sale locally. Happy now?" Dad beamed.

Katie nodded blissfully, but Jess was staring at the table, twisting her fingers together. "I still think Misty's going to hate it," she muttered. She looked anxiously over at Misty, snoozing by the kitchen radiator on her favorite pink blanket. It had been Jess's when she was little, and Misty had adopted it.

"What sort of dog should we get?" Katie asked, ignoring her grumpy big sister. She wished she could remember the puppy in her dream better.

"Nothing too big!" Mom said quickly.

"But not too small, either. We want to be able to go on some good long walks." Dad sounded as though he was really looking forward to it. "How about a terrier? An Airedale—they're great dogs, really friendly."

"I've always liked pugs," Mom said thoughtfully.

"The ones with the squished-up faces?" Katie asked, giggling.

Mom nodded. "I like the way their tails curl up," she said, smiling. "What about you, Katie? This was your idea. What kind of dog would you like?"

Katie thought back to her dream. "What sort of dog has long ears?" she asked, wrinkling her nose as she tried to remember more. "A brown and white puppy with long ears. I dreamed about one like that last night."

Jess sniffed, as though she thought that was silly. "You can't get a dog because of a dream."

"Why not?" Mom asked gently. "Katie's been thinking about it a lot, Jess. That's probably why she dreamed about a puppy."

"Maybe it was a spaniel?" Dad suggested. He got up and disappeared into the living room. They could hear him muttering to himself as he searched the bookcase, and he came back with Katie's dog sticker book. "Was he anything like this, Katie?"

Katie took the book and gasped with delight. There he was. A little brown and white dog, staring impishly out of the page at her, his eyes bright and alert. "A cocker spaniel," she murmured, reading the caption. "Oh, yes! I mean, I'd love any dog—even one with a squished face, Mom! But I'd really, really love one of those. . . ."

Chapter Three

A couple of days later, Katie was kneeling on the window seat in the living room, waiting for her dad to come home from work. As soon as she saw him walking down the road, she shot out of the front door and raced toward him.

"Hurry up, Dad, you're so late! I've been waiting forever!"

Her dad looked at his watch. "It's only six o'clock, Katie, that's the normal time I get home. Did your mom make a special dinner or something? What's the rush?"

"Oh, well, it feels later," Katie said excitedly. "We have to have dinner really quickly—we're going to see some cocker spaniel puppies! Mom found out about them, and the breeder only lives twenty minutes away!"

Luckily, Dad was as excited as she was, especially when he heard that Katie had seen pictures of the puppies on the breeder's website, and one of them was brown and white, exactly like the one in Katie's book. They both finished dinner long before Mom and Jess, and Katie glared at Mom when she started making a cup of coffee afterward.

"Mo-om!" she wailed. "We have to go! We said we'd be there by now!"

Jess was still slowly finishing her frozen yogurt, making each spoonful last, and Katie scowled at her, too. "You're doing that on purpose!" she said accusingly. "You don't even like frozen yogurt that much; you don't have to scrape it clean!"

"Go and put your coat on, Katie," Mom said. "We're obviously not going to get any peace until we go! Hurry up, Jess, you really are taking your time."

Jess huffed, but put the container in the garbage and went to get her coat, too. She looked like she was about to take a spelling test, not going to see a litter of gorgeous puppies.

"What's the matter?" Katie asked her in the back of the car. She was so excited about seeing the puppies, but Jess was sending out a black cloud of gloom right next to her. Katie couldn't ignore it. "Are you jealous?" she whispered. "You're being so grumpy."

Jess looked like she might snap back, but then she sighed. "No. I'm just worried about Misty, that's all."

"She might like having a dog to make friends with," Katie suggested hopefully.

But Jess looked doubtful. "We'll see," she murmured.

The puppies were just as cute as Katie had imagined they would be.

The breeder's house had a sunroom at the back, which was being used as a puppy room. Katie could hear the puppies squeaking and yapping as soon as she got to the front door.

Mrs. Jones, the breeder, laughed at Katie, who was hopping up and down with impatience as Mom and Dad followed her into the hall. "Come and see them," she said, leading everyone to the back room. The door was blocked off with a knee-high board to keep the puppies in their own space. They were tumbling around all over the room, while their mother watched them from a comfortable cushion.

Katie couldn't see the little brown and white puppy she'd loved from the website. "There was one brown and white boy puppy in the photos. Is he already gone?" she asked anxiously.

Mrs. Jones looked around the room. "Goodness, where has he gone? He's the silliest of them all. Ah!" She smiled and pointed. "Look! See that big cardboard tube?"

Katie nodded. The tube was wriggling, and as she watched, a little brown nose appeared at one end, followed by some stubby whiskers and a pair of sparkling dark brown eyes. The brown and white puppy popped out of the tube and stared curiously at the visitors.

"Oh, he's gorgeous!" Katie giggled.

"Do you want to go in and play with them?" Mrs. Jones asked.

"Yes, please!" Katie said eagerly.

"Are they okay with meeting strangers?" Dad asked.

"They're quite friendly," Mrs. Jones replied.

"Well, remember to be really gentle, Katie," said Dad.

Soon Katie's whole family was sitting on the floor, with puppies sniffing and licking and climbing over them. Even Jess couldn't resist the cuddly little things. There were only five puppies, but there seemed to be way more since they all wriggled and darted around so quickly. The brown and white puppy was definitely in charge—or at least he thought he was. Katie watched him hopefully. She really wanted to pick him up, but she didn't want to scare him.

The puppy gave her an interested look. She smelled nice. Very friendly.

Katie gently held out the back of her hand for him to sniff, and he crept up to her, his tail wagging slowly. He sniffed her fingers, then butted them lovingly with his nose.

"Your nose is cold," Katie whispered. She ran her fingers over his silky, domed head. His fur was so soft.

The puppy blissfully closed his eyes and rested his chin on Katie's knee. That was *very* nice.

"He's a beauty," Dad murmured. "What do you think, Katie?
Is this the one?"

Chapter Four

There was a lot to do before Katie and her family could bring the puppy home. Katie, Jess, and their mom went to the pet shop on the way home from school the next day, with a long list. Katie had brought all of her allowance with her, although she didn't have much left after buying Christmas presents. It certainly wasn't enough to buy everything she wanted to get for their new puppy.

"Katie! Come and choose a collar and leash," Mom called from the counter. Katie stopped trying to choose between a squeaky fish and a bright orange nylon bone, and ran over.

"What color do you think?" Mom said thoughtfully. "This blue one is nice."

Katie nodded. "Ye-es . . . But don't you think he'd look better with a red collar? It would show up really well against his brown and white fur." She lifted out the bright collar and held it up.

Mom added the red collar and leash to the pile on the counter—a sleeping cushion, a big bag of puppy food, and food and water bowls. "Did you find a toy for him, Katie? And where's Jess? Did she want to get anything?"

"She's choosing a Christmas present for Misty. I'll get her. And I've *almost* decided which toys."

Katie managed to limit herself to three dog toys, and five minutes later they were walking home, loaded with bags.

"There's one thing missing, girls. We still need to think what we're going to call the puppy. Ow, this food is heavy!" Mom shifted the bag to her other hand.

"I've been thinking about it!" Katie hitched up the big purple cushion they'd chosen for the puppy to sleep on. The man in the shop had said some puppies liked to chew baskets, so cushions were better. "I think he really looks like a Timmy. Sort of silly but cute." She looked anxiously at Mom and Jess.

"Timmy . . . Yes, I like it," Mom said.

Jess just shrugged. Even though she'd enjoyed cuddling the puppies at Mrs. Jones's house, she still wasn't sure that they should actually get one. "It's okay," she muttered.

Back at home, Katie wandered around the kitchen, trying out the cushion and bowls in different positions.

"Katie, I'm not cooking with a dog cushion in front of the oven," Mom pointed out. "Try by the radiator: That'll be nice and warm."

Katie pushed Misty's blanket out of the way, and stood back and looked at the cushion. "That's perfect!" she declared happily.

Misty prowled in from the hallway and stopped. Someone had put a big purple cushion exactly in her favorite sleeping spot. She stalked over and stared up at Katie accusingly.

"Hi, Misty!" Katie bent down to stroke her. "Look, this is where your new friend's going to sleep. He's a puppy named Timmy. He's so sweet, and I bet you'll love him!"

Misty climbed onto her fleecy pink blanket and sat down, squishing herself in beside the vast cushion. She glared at it disapprovingly. What was going on?

Katie didn't notice. She was looking at the calendar on the wall and wishing it wasn't so long until they brought Timmy home. "Another three whole days till Saturday!" She sighed. "That's forever!"

The brown and white puppy gazed thoughtfully up at the window. It was only very slightly open, but the most delicious smells kept floating through it. Fresh air and frosty ground and general outsideness. It smelled *wonderful*. The puppies weren't allowed outside yet, as they were too young, but the brown and white puppy was desperate to explore. Where were all those delicious smells coming from?

He looked around. His brothers and sisters were snoozing in their basket, and their mother was half-asleep, too. If he went for a little exploring now, probably nobody would notice. . . .

Mrs. Jones had left the window open to air out the room, but she'd carefully made sure it was only open a crack. Not that the puppies were big or strong enough to get up onto the windowsill, of course! They were far too small for that.

The puppy looked up. Beneath the window was a chair. It was still too high for him to reach, but next to that was the old cardboard box Mrs. Jones had given them to play with. If he climbed onto that first, maybe he could jump onto the chair, and then to the window?

He scrambled onto the box, tiny claws scrabbling. Then he made the next hop onto the chair. Hmmm. It was still a long way to the windowsill. But . . .

"Oh, you naughty little thing!" Mrs. Jones was half laughing, half concerned as she rescued the brown and white puppy, who was standing on the chair seat, his paws on the back, staring up at the open window

hopefully. "You could have really hurt yourself. And I suppose you were going for the window. I'd better shut that." She smiled. "I think your new family should call you Rascal. You're going to be a real little handful!"

On Saturday morning, Katie woke up early with a wonderful feeling of excitement. She was still sleepy, and it took her a couple of minutes to work out why she was feeling so happy. It was the first day of Christmas vacation, but there was something more. . . . Then she remembered. They were getting Timmy today! She bounced out of bed and flung on her clothes.

She clattered downstairs, wondering where everyone else was. Misty stared at her reproachfully as she banged the kitchen door open, then turned around on her blanket and settled down with her back to Katie.

Katie was aching with impatience by the time the rest of the family got up.

She couldn't understand how Dad could sit there with the paper and drink a cup of coffee so slowly.

"When are we going to *go*?" she wailed, standing in the kitchen doorway with her coat on.

"It only takes twenty minutes to get there in the car," Mom pointed out.

Katie frowned. "But it takes at least five minutes to get *in* the car! It's rude to be late, Mom, you're always saying that."

"Well, that still leaves us half an hour." Dad folded up the paper. "Anyone else want more toast?"

"Oh!" Katie groaned, and stomped out of the room.

At Mrs. Jones's
house, the
puppies
were
playing
a silly
game with
the big cardboard tube. It was wide
enough for them to get inside now, and
they were scrabbling through it, nipping
at one another's tails.

Suddenly, there was a scratching,
scuffling noise from inside the tube as
the brown and white puppy shot out of
one end. He shook his ears to unsquish
them, then trotted hopefully over to
Mrs. Jones. "What is it, boy? Oh, there's
the doorbell." She smiled down at the
puppy. "Did you hear the car? Someone

special's coming for you!"

When Mrs. Jones answered the door, Katie had to stop herself from dashing into the house and hugging the puppy —she was already thinking of him as Timmy. But she knew she shouldn't. He was still little, and he probably wouldn't remember who she was. She would have to be really calm and gentle. But it was so hard when she was this excited!

Katie walked into the living room, digging her nails into the palms of her hands. Would Timmy even remember her?

The puppies were all standing by the sunroom door, watching to see who was coming. Suddenly, there was a piercing squeak of a bark, and a small brown and white ball of fur hurled itself at the board across the door, scrabbling madly. Two little white paws clawed their way over the top, and Timmy flung himself over the board, heading for Katie as fast as he could. He knew that girl! She was the one who'd cuddled him!

"Oh, my goodness!" Mrs. Jones exclaimed. "None of them has ever done that before." She hurried forward. "Is he all right?"

Timmy was shaking himself dazedly— it had been a long way down for such a small dog—but then he barked again and ran to Katie.

Katie knelt down and hugged him to her lovingly. "Oh, Timmy. You remembered me!"

Chapter Five

Mrs. Jones had given them a special box for carrying Timmy home. Katie was disappointed—she'd been looking forward to cuddling him in the car—but Mom said it might be dangerous if he wriggled out of her arms. He'd feel safer in the box.

Katie wasn't so sure. She hated hearing the snuffling, whimpering noises that

Timmy was making behind her seat. He didn't sound happy at all.

"So when we get home, we're going to let Timmy out into the kitchen, girls. That's the plan," Mom reminded them. "He needs to get used to the house slowly. Remember, he's only been used to staying in the puppy room. The whole house would be overwhelming for him. And then we need to introduce him to Misty very carefully."

"Can I show him my bedroom?" Katie asked hopefully.

"I wouldn't just yet," Dad told her, as they turned onto their road. "For a start, the mess would probably give him a heart attack. . . ."

Katie grinned. That was true. Timmy could easily get lost in there. As soon as the car stopped, she struggled out of her seat belt, her fingers clumsy with excitement, and gently lifted Timmy's box out of the back. She could feel him skidding around inside, even though she was walking so slowly and carefully. "We'll get you out in just a minute," she whispered. "You can see your new home!"

Katie carried Timmy into the house and put the box down on the kitchen floor, kneeling beside it. Then she undid the flaps that held its cover together. Timmy stared up at her, puzzled by his strange, dark journey. But then he recognized Katie and gave a pleased little whine, scrabbling at the cardboard with his claws to show her he wanted to get out.

"Come on, Timmy!" Katie lifted him out, and cuddled him lovingly. He was staring at her, his big, dark eyes bright and interested. Then all at once he reached up and licked Katie's chin, making her splutter and giggle.

"Well, I don't mind if you do that, but I wouldn't do it to Mom," she whispered to him.

Timmy gazed at her lovingly. He was confused about what was going on—his brothers and sisters weren't here, and neither was his mom, but if he was going to get cuddled and played with, maybe it would be all right.

He wondered if there were any other dogs here. He couldn't smell them, but there was another smell, a different smell that he didn't recognize. . . .

"How's he doing, Katie?" Dad had come in from the car. He and Mom and Jess had been chatting with the lady next door, telling her about their new arrival.

"I'm just about to show him his cushion and his food bowl," Katie explained. She walked around the kitchen with Timmy, holding him up to see out the back door. Then she put him down gently next to his cushion. "This is where you're going to sleep. Look."

Mom came in holding Timmy's collar and leash. "Don't forget these, Katie. Remember what the website said—we need to keep him on the leash in case we have to stop him from chasing Misty."

"Oh, yes!" Katie bent down and fastened the bright red collar around Timmy's neck. "Very nice!" she said. She clipped on the leash and Timmy looked at it in surprise. What was this? Oh, a leash, like his mom had.

He sniffed at the big, purple cushion, and sneezed.

Dad laughed. "It probably smells too clean. Don't worry, Timmy, it'll be nice and doggy in a couple of days."

Just then, Jess came in carrying Misty. She'd gone to fetch her from upstairs. Misty spent most of her time snoozing on Jess's bed.

Timmy was delighted. He peered up at Misty, his whiskers twitching. So that was what the interesting smell he'd noticed was! A friend! He danced clumsily over to her on his too-big puppy paws, and barked cheerfully to say hello. Katie followed, holding his leash and watching cautiously.

The fur on Misty's back stood up straight, and her tail fluffed up to twice its normal size. She hissed warningly. *Stay away!*

"Timmy . . ." Katie said anxiously, but Timmy wasn't listening. He had no experience with cats, so he didn't recognize Misty's warning for what it was. He just wanted to say hello to this big, fluffy animal.

Misty hissed again, then yowled and spat, her ears laid right back against her head.

Timmy stared at her, feeling very confused. Then he backed up a little. He didn't understand what was going on, but he could tell now that something was wrong. He looked up at Katie and whimpered, asking for help.

"I told you she'd hate it!" Jess said accusingly to Mom. "Oh, Misty, no!" Misty had jumped out of her arms, and was prowling across the kitchen toward Timmy.

Katie was just stooping to pick him up when Misty pounced and swiped her paw across Timmy's nose—not very hard, just enough to make it clear she really wanted him gone.

Timmy howled in surprise and dismay. His nose did hurt, but it was more the shock of it that upset him so much. He'd played rough games with his brothers and sisters, but no one had ever scratched him before. He buried his nose in Katie's sweater as she picked him up, and snuffled miserably.

Misty hissed at him triumphantly, her fur still bristling.

"That was so mean of Misty!" Katie cried angrily. "All he did was try to say hello, and she clawed him! His nose is bleeding!" She snuggled Timmy close and glared at Jess and Misty.

"Maybe we should put Timmy's cushion in the pantry to start off with," Dad said worriedly, looking at Timmy's nose. "I think it's a lot for Misty to get used to all at once."

Jess folded her arms and stared at the ceiling. "I told you this was a bad idea," she said. "Misty hates dogs, and this is her home. It's *never* going to work."

"Well, now it's Timmy's home, too!" Katie snapped back. "Misty's just going to have to get used to it."

Katie sat up on her bed in the dark, her blanket wrapped around her shoulders, listening anxiously as Timmy let out another mournful howl. Everyone had agreed that he would stay in the kitchen and the pantry at first, so he could get used to the house gradually. It was what all the dog books and websites had suggested, especially as Timmy was still learning to ask to go outside if he needed to. Mom really didn't want him messing up all the carpets.

Mom and Dad had been careful to keep Misty away from Timmy for the rest of the day, after their fight. For tonight, they'd put a litter tray in the hall, and Misty was sleeping on Jess's bed, as she always did. Katie had begged her parents to let Timmy sleep in her room, too, just for his first night, but Mom had said definitely not.

Timmy just didn't understand why he

couldn't explore the rest of the house. Katie had stayed in the kitchen almost all that day, playing with him and cuddling him, but Timmy had still been curious about what was going on everywhere else.

That cat was allowed to go wherever she liked, but he had to stay in, except when he was taken into the yard. It didn't seem fair. And when she wanted to be in the kitchen to eat her food, he had to go into the pantry! Why couldn't he eat with her? She might even have leftovers.

But the worst thing was that now they'd all gone to bed. He had to sleep in the kitchen, and he was all on his own! It was so lonely! Where was everyone?

He howled so much that Katie just

couldn't get to sleep. She sat there listening to the sorrowful wails from downstairs, and eventually she couldn't bear it any longer. She crept out of bed, wrapping her blanket around her like a cloak and trailing it along behind her. Mom might have said Katie absolutely must not have Timmy in her room, but she hadn't said anything about not sleeping in the kitchen with Timmy, had she?

Timmy was sitting on his cushion, staring anxiously into the darkness. Like all dogs, he could see well in the dark, but he wasn't used to being all alone— he never had been before. What if Katie never came back? He didn't want to be on his own forever! Timmy whimpered again, and then stopped. He could hear footsteps, and an odd swishing noise.

What was that?

He looked worriedly at the door, hoping it wasn't something horrible. Maybe the cat was coming to be mean to him again. In his mind, she was about twice her real size, and her tail was enormous. Maybe that was what the strange noise was. . . . Timmy whined nervously.

Katie hitched up her trailing blanket and gently pushed the door open. She called softly to him. "Timmy? Hey, sweetie!"

Timmy heaved a massive sigh of relief and trotted over to her.

"O o o p s !" Katie giggled. "I

just walked into a chair! It's so dark."

Timmy woofed in agreement. Dark, and lonely. He gazed hopefully up at her.

"Look, I've brought my blanket. I've come to keep you company. You're used to having your mom to sleep with, aren't you?" Katie curled up next to Timmy's cushion, and Timmy snuggled gratefully into her lap. This was much better.

Katie smiled down at him as he dozed off into a deep puppy sleep. He was hers, at last! The kitchen floor was chilly, and she had pins and needles in her toes, but she didn't care. It was worth it.

Chapter Six

Katie's mom came downstairs on Sunday morning and found them both curled up together, Katie with her head on Timmy's cushion, and Timmy snuggled under the blanket with her.

"Katie! I thought you were still in bed! Actually, I was surprised you weren't up and playing with Timmy already." Mom sighed as she poured Katie some juice and filled Timmy's food bowl. "I should have known."

Katie grinned. "Sorry, Mom. He was so lonely. I listened to him whining and crying, and I just couldn't bear it any longer."

"The thing is, now he'll expect you to do it again tonight." Mom watched as Timmy wolfed down his breakfast. "You can't sleep on the kitchen floor every night, Katie!"

Katie wriggled her shoulders. "I know. This floor's really hard. Honestly, Mom, I won't do it again. I think he was just miserable the first night, that's all."

Katie was right. Timmy had never been left alone before, and he hadn't been sure that anyone would ever come back for him. Now that he knew that

Katie and the rest of the family weren't far away, and he'd see them in the morning, he didn't mind being alone so much.

In fact, on Sunday night, he was so worn out from playing in the yard with Katie for most of the day that he curled up on his cushion and fell asleep almost as soon as Katie went to bed. He didn't bother with even one little howl.

A couple of days later, Katie's parents decided that Timmy had settled in so well that they could let him explore more of the house.

"Just downstairs," Dad said. "There's so much stuff he could accidentally damage upstairs. Imagine if he started chewing your mom's shoe collection. She'd never forgive him!"

Katie nodded, though she wished she could have Timmy in her room. Still, she was really looking forward to curling up with him to watch TV in the living room.

"Come on, Timmy," she called, standing by the kitchen door and patting her knees. "Come on, boy!"

Timmy looked at her with his head to one side. He wasn't quite sure what was happening. He wasn't allowed out of that door, was he? He'd been told *no* when he tried before. He pattered slowly over to Katie, then turned and looked at her mom, waiting to see if she'd yell at him.

Mom laughed. "It's okay, Timmy. Go on, go with Katie."

Timmy woofed with excitement, and trotted happily into the hallway. New things to smell! He worked his way curiously along Katie's and Jess's school bags and shoes, which were by the front door, then poked his nose into the living room. Jess was sitting on the sofa reading a magazine, with Misty on her lap.

Over the last couple of days, Katie and Jess and Mom and Dad had very carefully kept Timmy and Misty apart. They wanted to give Timmy time to settle down, and Misty needed to get used to the idea of a dog in the house.

Misty had spent as much time as she possibly could in Jess's room, only coming into the kitchen to scarf down her food—with one watchful eye on the pantry door the whole time. She would then shoot out of the cat flap, and rely on Jess letting her in the front door when she wanted to come in again. Now she looked up at Timmy and hissed.

"Oh, Misty!" Katie sighed. "Don't be so grumpy."

Timmy had almost forgotten his first meeting with the cat. He was very little, and he was naturally friendly. He assumed everyone else was, too. He bounced over toward Misty and Jess, his tail wagging, and yapped excitedly at her. Misty shot onto the arm of the sofa and growled, her back arching.

Timmy's tail drooped, and he looked

around at Katie. He was only trying to be friendly. *Why doesn't she like me?*

"Keep him away from Misty," Jess said irritably. "He's upsetting her."

"Mom said we could watch TV," Katie said. "There's a safari show on; I thought Timmy could watch it with me. Anyway, Misty and Timmy have to learn to get along. If we can just get them used to being in the same room, that would be really good."

"I suppose . . ." Jess muttered. "Just keep an eye on him, though!"

For the next half hour, Misty glowered from the arm of the sofa, her tail twitching warningly, and Timmy shot her curious, sidelong glances from the armchair, where he was curled up on Katie's lap.

Gradually, Misty started to relax, and after a while she dozed off on the sofa arm, with one eye half open.

Timmy sat quietly for a while, but

soon he began to feel restless. He slipped down from Katie's knee and went exploring. This was much more exciting! Katie was half watching him, but the little lion cubs on the show were so cute!

Timmy sniffed his way around the room, investigating behind the Christmas tree and sneezing at the dust under the big bookcase. He even managed to wriggle under the sofa. It was dark, and it smelled interesting. He could pop his head out from underneath as well, and then hide again, which made Katie giggle. It was a good game.

He crawled the whole length of the sofa, and poked his nose out at Jess's end. There was an interesting fluffy thing there, dangling down and twitching gently.

Timmy was mesmerized. It went to and fro, waving at him. The fluffy thing was like one of the toys Katie had given him, a furry rat that squeaked. Maybe this one would squeak, too, if he bit it? He wriggled a little farther out from under the sofa, just as Katie realized she hadn't seen him for a minute or so.

"Where's Timmy? Is he behind the sofa? Oh, Timmy, no!"

And Timmy pounced on Misty's tail. . . .

Chapter Seven

Misty shot up in the air with a screech, and Timmy howled in shock—he hadn't expected the fluffy toy to do *that*. . . . He peered nervously from under the sofa just as Misty raced out of the room. Why was she so upset? Perhaps it was *her* fluffy toy?

"Oh, Timmy..." Katie said worriedly. She was trying to sound angry, but she couldn't help a tiny smile—Misty had looked so funny, like something out of a cartoon, when she'd leaped into the air.

"I'm telling Mom!" Jess snapped. "He did that on purpose, and you weren't watching him!" Then she ran after Misty.

Katie picked Timmy up. "Oh, Timmy. That was her tail. I don't think you knew that, though, did you? You didn't do it on purpose; I know you didn't. Our plan to get you and Misty to like each other isn't going very well, is it . . ."

And things got worse and worse over the next week. Rather than Misty and Timmy getting used to each other as time went on, Misty just got more and more furious about her peaceful home being invaded. She tried as hard as she could to keep away from Timmy, but she couldn't escape from him. It seemed that wherever she went, there he was, too.

Timmy didn't understand that Misty wanted to be left alone. She kept running off upstairs whenever he tried to play with her, and when he tried to follow he got in trouble.

He was allowed out on his own in the yard now, though, and he thought he'd had a stroke of luck one afternoon when he found Misty snoozing on the garden bench in a patch of winter sunlight—she couldn't dash away up the stairs now! But she raced up to the top of the apple tree and snarled at him while he barked hopefully. Eventually, he gave up and ran over to Katie, who was calling him in.

Back in the kitchen, Timmy lay quietly on Katie's lap, even though she bounced his squeaky ball for him. His ears were drooping and he rested his nose on his paws, gazing sadly at the back door.

"You really want her to play with you, don't you?" Katie sighed. "I think Misty's too old for playing, Timmy."

Timmy heard the worry in her voice and rubbed his head against her arm lovingly.

But Katie was right. Misty was an old cat, and stubborn. She didn't like new things, and she found it so strange and upsetting having Timmy around that she didn't even want to eat anymore. Besides, her food was in the kitchen, where he was. It was easier just not to bother. As the days went by, she started to look thinner.

A few days before Christmas, Timmy was curled up on his cushion, feeling bored. Katie had left him in the kitchen, explaining that she had to go upstairs and wrap presents in her room, because they were a secret and no one was supposed to see. Timmy still wasn't allowed upstairs, but she promised she'd be back soon.

Katie had shut the kitchen door when she went upstairs, but Timmy had been practicing, and he could claw it open unless it was shut really tight. Timmy hooked his claws into the crack and scrabbled until it clicked open. Then he trotted cheerfully out. He was so clever! Katie had been gone for a while. He was sure she wouldn't mind if he went to find her, would she?

Timmy headed for the stairs, and suddenly felt a little less clever. They were very big. He almost couldn't see the top. But he knew Katie would be up there. He could smell her, and as a tracking dog, his sense of smell was excellent.

He heaved himself up onto the first step, which wasn't too difficult, except there were a lot more of them before he got to the top. It took him ten minutes to get all the way up, and he nearly went back to his comfy cushion several times.

But the exciting new smells upstairs soon made him forget how hard it had been to get there, and he set off snuffling along the carpet. Ah! An open door! Maybe Katie was here. No, it didn't smell like Katie. But there was Misty, curled up asleep on the pink bedspread. Timmy trotted eagerly into the room. He was delighted to see her. If he woke her, perhaps she would play with him. He stood up with his front paws on the edge of the bed and licked

Misty's nose. He could only just reach.

Misty was sleeping peacefully, knowing *that dog* was downstairs and she didn't need to worry. Then she woke up with a sudden fright.

He was right there! There, in Jess's room! Was nowhere safe anymore? Misty leaped off the bed and raced across the room, looking for a way to escape. Timmy was whining, trying to show her he was friendly, but all Misty could see was Timmy in the one place she'd felt was safe. Desperately, she clawed her way up Jess's curtains, and up onto the top of the wardrobe.

The scuffling and barking brought Jess running upstairs; Katie rushed in after her.

"He's not allowed in here!" Jess

yelled. "Get him out of my room! Misty, it's okay, come on down, kitty, kitty . . ." She turned back to Katie, who was standing by the door, looking horrified. "Come on, get him out!" she cried angrily.

Timmy flinched back. Jess was so angry with him, and Misty was cowering on top of the wardrobe. . . . It had all gone wrong! He'd only been trying to be friendly. And now he was in trouble again!

Katie scooped him up and hurried downstairs. "Oh, Timmy! What were you doing up there? You can't chase Misty, it's mean!"

Katie sounded mad, Timmy thought miserably. He sighed. He hadn't meant to be naughty.

"What's going on up there?" Mom was standing at the bottom of the stairs looking worried.

"Katie let Timmy get into my room, and now Misty's stuck on top of my wardrobe!" Jess yelled from upstairs. "Mom, we have to shut him in the kitchen so Misty can calm down; it's just not fair."

"Oh, Katie. Did he upset Misty again?"

Timmy whined sadly as he heard another angry voice.

"Jess is right, Katie," Mom said firmly. "Put Timmy back in the kitchen, and make sure the door's shut tight. And hurry, Katie, we've got to finish the Christmas shopping this morning, remember. We need to get going."

"But Mom, he really doesn't like being shut in. . . ." Katie started to say, but Mom gave her a stern look, folding her arms. Katie sighed. "Sorry, Timmy. You have to go back in the kitchen. Stay here and be good, all right?"

Timmy watched, his big, dark eyes mournful, as she carefully shut the door. He was all alone, and everybody was angry with him. He howled miserably at the ceiling, then slumped on his cushion, listening to Katie and Jess and Mom in the hallway, getting ready to go out.

Timmy wriggled around sadly, trying to get comfortable. A piece of pink material was hanging on the radiator, and he knocked it down as he turned. It made him jump as it fell onto his

cushion. Timmy took
it in his mouth
to pull it out
of the way,
but he had
it tangled in
his paws, and
it tore a little. This was fun. . . .

The pink fabric was good to chew.
It made satisfying tearing noises as he
shredded it and shook it and rolled
around the floor with it. He felt much
better afterward, but quite tired. It had
been a busy morning climbing all those
stairs.

Timmy fell asleep, covered in small
bits of pink fleece.

A couple of hours later, Katie, Mom, and Jess came back. Timmy could hear them outside the kitchen and hopefully scratched the door a few times, but no one came to get him. He could hear Jess talking to Misty. *She* was allowed out. It wasn't fair. He trailed back to his cushion and nibbled a bit more on the pink fleece.

"Where's Misty's blanket, Mom?" Jess called. "It's not in my room, and you know she likes to sleep on it."

"Oh, I washed it, Jess, it was so dirty. It's hanging on the kitchen radiator to dry," Mom said.

Timmy could hear Jess coming toward the door, murmuring to Misty. "It's all right, we'll get your blanket, then you can have a nice nap."

As Jess opened the kitchen door, cuddling Misty, a guilty-looking brown and white puppy stared up at her, with shreds of pink blanket hanging out of the corners of his mouth.

Chapter Eight

Timmy lay on his cushion silently, only occasionally giving a sad little whine. Jess had been so angry, angrier than anyone had ever been with him before. She'd called him a bad dog, and lots of other horrible things. Even *Katie* had said he was naughty. He'd never heard her sound upset like that. And the worst thing was, they were right.

He *had* been naughty.

The kitchen door clicked open gently, and Katie came in, wearing her pajamas. Timmy looked up at her sadly. Was she still angry with him?

"Oh, Timmy. I'm sorry we shouted. You didn't know, did you? But Misty's really upset, Timmy, and Jess is *furious*." Katie sighed. "I thought you and Misty would learn to get along, but it just isn't happening." She stroked his ears gently, and Timmy laid his nose on her knee, gazing apologetically at her.

Katie looked guiltily around to the kitchen door, and then scooped him up in her arms. "Come on. We're both too miserable to be on our own. Mom and Dad have gone to bed, so I'm going to sneak you up to my room. We've got to be really quiet, because if anyone catches us, we'll be in big trouble, okay?"

Timmy snuggled gratefully into Katie's arms, and she tiptoed upstairs. She tucked him down beside her, and Timmy felt happy for the first time since Jess had been so mad. At least Katie still loved him.

But the next morning, Jess flung Katie's bedroom door open and rushed in, her face panicky.

Katie rolled over. "What is it?" she asked, too sleepy to remember that she should hide Timmy. Luckily, Jess seemed too distracted to notice him.

"Have you seen Misty?" she asked anxiously.

Katie shook her head, yawning.

"She didn't come back in last night! I was sure she'd be here this morning. She does stay out late sometimes, but never all night." She frowned at Katie. "You know why she's gone, don't you? Because of Timmy. He's driven her away, Katie!"

"That's not true—" Katie started to say, but Jess didn't let her finish.

"Of course it is! He eats her food, he chases her, he's bitten her tail, and now he's chewed up her most special thing! I'm just surprised she didn't leave before!"

Katie sat up in bed, carefully covering Timmy with the blanket. "Misty's just old and grumpy, and she's never been friendly to Timmy. She was the one who scratched him!"

"She's a cat, Katie! Cats don't like dogs! I told you and Mom and Dad that, and nobody listened, and now we've lost her. You were the one who wanted a dog in the first place. It's all your fault!"

"No, it isn't!" Katie yelled back, making Timmy tremble beside her. He hated shouting.

"It is, and stop trying to hide Timmy, because I know you've got him up here, and I'm telling Mom!" Jess stormed out, leaving Timmy whimpering.

"It's okay, boy," Katie muttered. "It'll be okay . . ."

But she wasn't at all sure that it would.

Katie and Timmy were in trouble. Jess was still claiming that Misty had run away because of Timmy. Katie had to admit it was true, but he hadn't been naughty on purpose. He was just being a dog—a friendly, bouncy, messy puppy.

He hadn't meant to upset Misty!

Dad had called their vet's office to tell them that Misty was missing. Misty had been microchipped, so that if anyone brought her into the vet's, they could tell at once who she belonged to. But Mom and Dad were sure that she would be back soon.

"It's only been one night, Jess," Mom said at breakfast, putting an arm around her.

Katie sat on the other side of the table, feeling miserable. She was worried about Misty, too, and Mom had yelled at her for having Timmy in her room. Now he was lying under the table, resting his nose on her feet. He could sense how upset everyone was, and it was horrible.

"She'll be back as soon as she gets hungry, Jess," Dad promised. "And it's the first morning of my vacation from work, remember, so I can help you look for her later if she doesn't turn up."

"It's only two days till Christmas!" Jess wailed. "What if Misty isn't back for Christmas Day?"

The problem was that Misty didn't want to be found. She was miserable, and she wanted to hide away from people, and especially from *dogs*. When she had seen her precious blanket in pieces all over the kitchen floor, she had known that she couldn't stay in the house any longer.

Misty had left home, and she wasn't coming back. Not while the dog was still there. She had plodded dismally through the yard, crawled under the back fence, and set off down the alleyway that led to the main road. She wanted to be far away, and by the time Jess had finished shouting at Katie and Timmy, and raced after her, Misty had gone too far to hear her frantic calling.

Misty liked being outdoors. She was good at hunting—she loved to give Jess mouse presents—and she adored sunbathing in the yard. Only now it was freezing, and she could smell snow in the air. And it felt different being outside all alone and knowing that she couldn't just slip back in through her cat flap to be safe and warm again.

She spent the night huddled under a garden shed, a few streets away from her own house. It was horrible; still, she couldn't go back. But when she awoke in the morning, hungry and stiff with cold, Misty wished that Jess was there to cuddle her, and open one of her favorite cans of food for breakfast. Maybe she should go home, just to eat. Then she could leave again, after she'd seen Jess. . . .

Misty crawled out of the grubby little den she'd found and sniffed the air anxiously. Home was—which way?

In a sudden panic, Misty leaped onto the top of a garden wall, looking worriedly around. She didn't know! She had been so desperate to get away yesterday that she hadn't tried to remember. Now all the yards looked the same, and none of them was hers. . . .

Chapter Nine

It was the saddest Christmas Day ever. The whole family was sitting in the living room with the Christmas tree lights on, trying to be enthusiastic about presents. Carols were playing, and it looked like a perfect Christmas scene. Even Timmy had tinsel around his collar. But there was a cat-shaped hole where Misty should have been, perched on the back of the sofa, waiting to pounce on the crackly wrapping paper. Everyone was thinking about her.

"Your turn, Jess!" Mom said brightly.

Jess stared at the pile of gifts in front of her as though she wasn't really seeing them. She was holding a plastic package in her hands, with a picture on it that looked very much like Misty. Katie looked over at her miserably. She'd been with Jess at the pet shop when she'd bought it—the fancy cat "chocolates" that were supposed to have been Misty's Christmas present.

Tears started to seep out of the corners of Jess's eyes, and Mom sighed. "Let's leave the rest of the presents till later."

Dad stood up. "Come on, Katie, it's time

for Timmy's best Christmas present!"

Katie nodded. She and Dad had planned a while ago to take Timmy for his first walk on Christmas Day. Katie had been looking forward to it ever since they got Timmy—they'd had to wait until he'd had all his vaccinations before he could go out and meet other dogs. They were going to take him just as far as the park near Katie and Jess's school, so as not to tire him out too much. "Timmy, walk, come on!"

Timmy raced to the front door, leaping excitedly around Katie's legs, squeaking and whining with delight. They were going out! Katie had his leash. He'd seen other dogs at his old house with leashes on, and he knew it meant a walk.

"Timmy, calm down! Shhh! Look, if you don't keep still, I won't even be able to get it on you!" Katie was half laughing, half serious. She was trying to clip the leash to Timmy's collar, but he kept licking her hand and barking, and then rushing to scrabble at the door.

Katie's dad grabbed his coat, and stuffed a handful of papers into his pocket.

"What are they?" Katie asked.

Her dad sighed. "Just some more posters. I promised Jess."

"Oh . . ." Katie nodded. Suddenly, the excitement about their first walk faded a little. Jess had papered their neighborhood with LOST posters over the last couple of days, but no one had called to say they'd seen a fluffy gray cat.

Katie wondered if she should go and ask Jess if she should take some, too, but Jess still wasn't speaking to her.

Timmy looked up at them and whined again. He felt the change in Katie, that suddenly she wasn't happy anymore. He guessed it was because of Misty—everyone was unhappy about her. He missed her, too, even though she would never play with him. He hung his head sadly.

Jess wandered into the hallway, followed by Mom, who was looking at her watch. "I need to prepare the roast potatoes and salad. You go with them, Jess. You can't sit around all day. I know you don't want to, but honestly, getting some fresh air will make you feel better."

"Oh, Mom, no . . ." Jess murmured.

"I mean it, Jess. Go and get your coat on." Mom gave Jess a quick hug, and a gentle push in the direction of the door. "Go!"

Even Jess trailing along in a miserable cloud couldn't stop Timmy from dancing around and winding his leash around Katie's legs as they headed out the front door. There was so much to see, so many delicious new smells. He was sure there must be at least a hundred other dogs on this street; he could smell them all! Timmy suddenly stopped, nearly tripping Katie with his leash.

"I think Timmy might need some obedience classes soon," Dad said, laughing.

Katie tried to coax him to move, but Timmy wasn't listening. He'd had a brilliant idea. He could smell all those dogs, so clearly. He was *good* at smelling things. So maybe he could sniff out Misty! He bounded ahead, his nose busily at work. There were lots of cat smells, too. . . .

Misty was hiding out behind a big, smelly garbage can, in a tiny yard behind a row of shops on the way to Katie and Jess's school.

It was horrible. There were rats, and although Misty liked to hunt mice, the rats were not the same thing at all. They were big and frightening. She was huddled inside a tattered cardboard box, and every so often a rat would scurry past. The only good thing about the yard was that there was a lot of food around, although it wasn't as nice as the special food Jess gave her.

Jess . . . Misty got up and turned around anxiously. She didn't want to think about Jess. She missed Jess so much, but Jess didn't care about her anymore. Jess had let a dog into the house. Even into Misty and Jess's room. That wasn't Misty's home now. Jess didn't love her anymore.

But what was she going to do? Another rat scuttled past, baring its teeth at Misty. She couldn't stay here, but she had no idea where to go. *I need a new home*, Misty thought miserably. *But I don't want one. I want my old home back!*

And I'd even share it with that dog, if it meant I could still be with Jess. . . .

Timmy was the only one enjoying the walk. He danced around, snuffling and scrabbling happily as they reached the shops, and all those interesting smells. There were definitely cats here, too.

Jess was silent, trudging along with her head down— except when they happened to see a cat, when she'd look up hopefully, then sigh and stare at the pavement again.

"I think it's going to snow." Dad was looking up at the sky. "The clouds have got that yellowish look. And it's certainly cold enough. I'm freezing. Should we turn back, girls?"

"Mmm. Come on, Timmy." Katie tugged gently on his leash. But Timmy wasn't listening. He was straining forward against the leash, looking excited. Then he turned and gazed anxiously at Katie, and uttered a sharp, urgent bark.

Can you smell what I smell?

"Timmy, we're going home, come on, boy."

No! Not now, we have to go this way!

"Tim-my!" Katie's voice was starting to sound angry.

Timmy looked worriedly up at her. How could he make her understand? He had a horrible feeling she wasn't going to. But he was sure he recognized that smell and he had to investigate. . . . Timmy gave Katie an apologetic look with his big, dark eyes, and moved a step toward her, loosening his leash.

"Good boy, Timmy," Katie said in a relieved voice.

Then Timmy jumped back suddenly, dragging his leash out of Katie's hand, and dashed away down a little alley, following that familiar scent. Now where was it coming from . . . ?

Katie stared down at her hand for a second, as though expecting the leash to still be in it. Then she raced after Timmy, calling anxiously to him.

"Katie! Timmy!" Dad had been staring at the snow clouds, and looked back just in time to see Katie vanishing down the alley, too.

Timmy bounded into the little yard, trailing his leash, and stopped, looking around. Now that he was here, there were lots of other smells, too—old food, and strange animal smells that he wasn't sure about. But yes . . . there was a definite hint of Misty's scent as well. She was this way. He trotted over to the garbage cans, poking his nose between them hopefully. Yes! There she was! Curled up in an old cardboard box, and staring fearfully back at him.

Timmy barked for joy. He'd found her! He called excitedly for Katie to come, then rushed at Misty. He was just so glad to see her. Now everyone would be happy! He licked Misty's nose lavishly, and she shuddered and hissed, backing farther into the box. Timmy stepped back doubtfully. *Aren't you pleased to see me?*

Misty gave a sad little meow. Where *was* Jess? Maybe the dog could show her. She edged slowly out of the box, the fur on her spine slightly raised. *Don't lick me again,* she was telling Timmy. *But I'm not mad. Yet.*

Katie skidded into the yard, calling anxiously. "Timmy! Timmy, where are you?" She spotted his red leash, trailing out between the cans. "Oh, Timmy, are you eating something horrible?" She ran over, squeezing herself between the garbage cans, and Timmy stared up at her proudly.

Look! I've found her! he barked.

"What is it?" Katie asked, peering a little reluctantly into the box. She had a horrible feeling Timmy had found something yucky. "Misty! Oh, Misty!" Katie whirled around. "Jess, Jess, come here, quick!"

Jess and Dad were just following them up the alley. "You caught him," cried Dad. "Thank goodness."

"Yes, but look!" Katie picked Timmy up and hugged him lovingly. "Jess, come and see!" She stood back so Jess could get to the box. "Timmy's found her. He must have sniffed her out. That's why he ran off. He's so smart."

Jess dropped to her knees beside the box. "Misty!" she whispered.

Misty shot out of the box and Jess swooped down and picked her up.

Misty snuggled into Jess's coat, purring so hard her sides were shuddering.

"Katie, he found her!" Cradling Misty in her arms, Jess turned to her sister and Timmy. "I can't believe it. . . ."

Timmy reached out from Katie's arms, wriggling and wagging his tail happily, and amazingly, Misty didn't snarl or hiss at him. She shut her eyes slightly as he licked her nose. She didn't look as though she was enjoying it, but she let him.

"They're friends!" Katie said in amazement.

Misty glared at her, as if to say, *Don't push it. . . .*

But it was true. And above them, the first Christmas snowflakes were starting to float gently down.

"Misty, Timmy, turkey!" Katie laughed at Misty and Timmy, both standing eagerly by their food bowls. "Just a little; look, it's your Christmas dinner."

"Come on and eat yours, Katie,"

Mom said. "Dad's nearly finished."

"Don't worry, I'll be having seconds," Dad said with his mouth full.

Jess wasn't eating very much, either. Both girls just kept stopping and staring happily at Misty and Timmy wolfing down turkey.

"I hope Misty likes her new blanket," Katie said, ignoring the roast potato she was waving around.

"I bet she will. Look, she's about to try it out. It's a gorgeous present, Katie." Jess smiled at her, and Katie grinned back. It felt like the first time in weeks that Jess had smiled so easily at her. The angry wall between them seemed to have just crumbled away.

Misty prowled thoughtfully over to the new pink, fleecy blanket that lay neatly by the radiator. Katie had bought it weeks ago on a trip to the pet shop. She'd seen how old and tatty Misty's blanket had become, and had decided it was the perfect Christmas present.

Misty walked around it a couple of times, then graciously stepped onto it, testing it with her paws. She lay down—the picture of a comfy, turkey-fed cat, and purred.

Timmy finished licking the last possible taste of turkey out of his bowl, and gave Misty's bowl a quick lick just in case she'd left any. He sighed happily. Then he trotted over to Misty's blanket and gazed hopefully at her.

Misty gave him a resigned look. *If you must,* she seemed to be saying.

Katie and Jess watched, holding their breath, as Timmy whined eagerly and snuggled down next to Misty, putting his nose next to hers.

Misty put a firm paw on one of his long, curly, brown ears. Clearly, if Timmy was on her blanket, he had to keep still.

Timmy looked up at Katie lovingly and yawned. Two minutes later, both cat and puppy were fast asleep.

Jess put her arm around Katie's shoulder, and Katie smiled. It was a perfect Christmas after all.

Also available:

From the author of LOST IN THE SNOW

Max the Missing Puppy

Holly Webb

SCHOLASTIC

Ginger the Stray Kitten

Holly Webb

SCHOLASTIC

Sky the Unwanted Kitten

Holly Webb

SCHOLASTIC

Harry the Homeless Puppy

Holly Webb

SCHOLASTIC

Run, fly, or swim down to Grace's Pet Shop.

Lottie is happy to spend her time talking to the animals in her uncle's pet shop. Then one day, to her surprise, the animals start to talk back!

School is definitely more fun now that Lottie has a best friend, Ruby. But what will her new friend do if she finds out Lottie has magical powers?

A new neighbor is in town, with magic stronger than Lottie's and a mind to make trouble. Lucky for Lottie, the pet shop's newest resident, Giles the hamster, is ready to help.

Lottie has discovered an unhappy rabbit at a dingy pet shop. He seems to have budding magical abilities and Lottie is determined to rescue him!

Magic is everywhere and all the animals can talk!

THE PUPPY PLACE

SO MANY PERFECT PUPPIES - COLLECT THEM ALL!